The Faithfulness of Daniel

ALL IN ALL SERIES

Written by
Jalissa B. Pollard

Illustrated by
Adua Hernandez

Published by Melanin Origins

PO Box 122123; Arlington, TX 76012

Copyright 2022

First Edition

Series Editors: Reginald Robinson; Lenny Williams, & Shiree Fowler

Library of Congress Control Number: 2021942428

ISBN: 978-1-62676-507-8 hardback

ISBN: 978-1-62676-508-5 paperback

ISBN: 978-1-62676-509-2 ebook

This book is dedicated to the young men and women of the world who greet the light of each new day with courage and faith.

Jalissa B. Pollard

"Let me have and walk in an excellent spirit." - Daniel 6:3

Daniel was a man of deep faith who prayed three times a day, "Blessed is the name of God forever, who has wisdom and strength." Daniel 2:20

He was a bright young man, for God blessed Daniel with the gift of having dreams and explaining what they meant.

Because of his special gifts, Daniel became a wise and trusted leader for King Darius.

"But there is a God in heaven who uncovers mysteries." Daniel 2:28

Yet, although he always obeyed God's will, there were some people who grew jealous of Daniel and created a plan that would make it illegal for Daniel to pray to God.

The plan was to test Daniel's faithfulness by making him choose between obeying God's law or law of King Darius.

When King Darius noticed Daniel kept his relationship with God despite his strict orders, he punished Daniel by sending him into the lion's den.

Being treated wrongly by others is never a fun ordeal, but Daniel was not afraid for one moment. He trusted God; he knew that his God would take care of him.

And because of his faithfulness, God sent angels to shut the mouths of the lions while Daniel spent the night in the den.

Everyone was amazed to find that Daniel was well and unharmed the next morning. There was not a scratch on his body.

11

The story of Daniel reminds us that just as God rescued Daniel from the power of the lions, He has the power to rescue us from the scary things we may face.

All we have to do is be faithful - just like Daniel.

God rewards the faithful for obeying
His voice and keeping His laws.

Order Melanin Origins
ALL In All Series!

www.MelaninOrigins.com

CPSIA information can be obtained
at www.ICGtesting.com
Printed in the USA
JSHW012028220222
23220JS00003B/108